Say Hola to Spanish, Otra Vez

by Susan Middleton Elya • illustrated by Loretta Lopez

Lee & Low Books • New York

Printed in Hong Kong by South China Printing Co. (1988) Ltd.

Book Design by Christy Hale
Book Production by The Kids at Our House
Editorial consultant, Spanish language: Daniel Santacruz

The text is set in Benguiat, Frisky, La Bamba and Marguerita.
The illustrations are rendered in gouache and colored pencil on watercolor paper.

10 9 8 7 6 5 4 3 2
First Edition

Library of Congress Cataloging-in-Publication Data
Elya, Susan Middleton
Say hola to Spanish, otra vez/by Susan Middleton Elya; illustrated by Loretta Lopez.—1st ed.
p.   cm.
Continues: Say hola to Spanish.
Summary: Presents a humorous introduction to Spanish words through
illustrations and rhyming text.
ISBN 1-880000-83-0 (paperback)
1. Spanish language—Vocabulary—Juvenile literature. ×1. Spanish language—Vocabulary.U
I. Lopez, Loretta, ill. II. Title.
PC4445.E492 1997
428.1—dc21   97-6851
                                                                              CIP AC

To my dad for Spanish at suppertime
and to my mom for suggesting I write these books—With love, S.M.E.

For Mary, Paul, Nick, Micah (Mookie),
James, Mark and Noonie—Thank you—L.L.

Spanish is fun,
so give it a try.

¡Hola!

Hola
is hello,

¡Adiós!

adiós is good-bye.

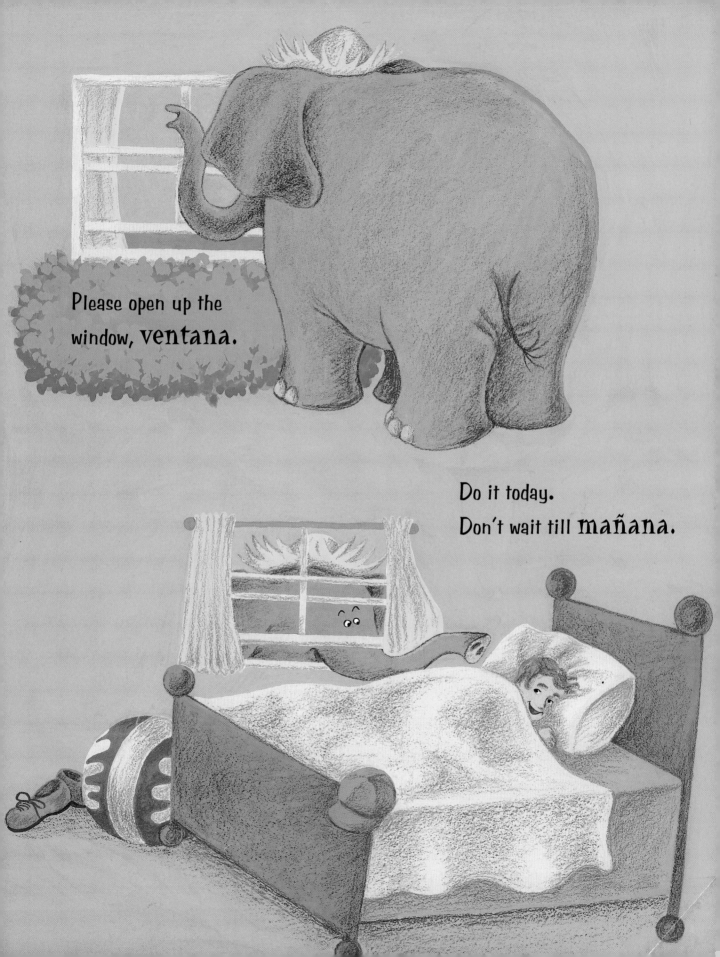

Please open up the window, **ventana**.

Do it today.
Don't wait till **mañana**.

In the cielo, see the cometa.

The procesión has a trompeta.

Musicians are **músicos**.

Flags are **banderas**.

Please don't run when using **tijeras**.

Guitars are **guitarras**,   tubas are **tubas**.

Naranjas are oranges;

grapes are called **uvas**.

These are **gusanos**.

Guisantes

are peas.

Don't say **gusanos**

when dining out, please.

There goes a **tigre**.

Here comes an **OSO**.

Safer in jaulas.

Less peligroso!

Let's buy some ice cream, yummy helado.

Too much makes you gordo instead of delgado.

There goes the **mosca**

around the **abeja**,

which stings the **gallina**,

which pecks the **oveja**.

A train is a tren,

plane—avión.

A bus—autobús;

a truck—camión.

Here is a **rata**,

here's a **ratón**.

There in the water!

A big **tiburón**!

A frog is a **rana**,

a toad is a **sapo**.

Neither one's known to be very **guapo**.

Take out your **lápiz**

and some **papel.**

You'll be an **artista**
someday, I can tell.

Let's ride the barco

over the mar.

If it has a hole, we won't get too far.

Conejo is rabbit,

turtle—tortuga.

Both like to chomp on some lechuga.

Please take some fruit,

manzanas and fresas.

Or would you rather
enjoy hamburguesas?

Let's try a salad with tasty **tomate.**

After our meal, we'll drink **chocolate.**

Mountain is **montaña**.

Valley is **valle**.

Look both ways
when crossing the **calle**.

See the **juguetes**. A lovely **muñeca**.

Let's get some books
at the **biblioteca**.

It's getting late!
Check the **reloj**.

Rápidamente, it's time to go!

Don't forget the leche
at the mercado.

Oops! Too late!
The sign says cerrado.

Up in the sky, tonight's first **estrella**.

Look at the luna.
Tan grande, tan bella.

Hola is hello, adiós is good-bye.
Spanish is fun, so give it a try!

Glossary

abeja (ah-BEH-hah): bee

adiós (ah-dee-OCE): good-bye

artista (ahr-TEE-stah): artist

autobús (ow-toe-BOOCE): bus

avión (ah-vee-OHN): airplane

banderas (bahn-DEH-rahss): flags

barco (BAHR-koe): ship

biblioteca (bee-blee-oh-TEH-kah): library

calle (KAH-yeh): street

camión (kah-mee-OHN): truck

cerrado (seh-RRAH-doe): closed

chocolate (choe-koe-LAH-teh): hot chocolate

cielo (see-EH-loe): sky

cometa (koe-MEH-tah): comet

comida (koe-MEE-dah): food

conejo (koe-NEH-hoe): rabbit

cuchara (koo-CHAH-rah): spoon

delgado (del-GAH-doe): thin

estrella (es-TREH-yah): star

fresas (FREH-sahss): strawberries

gallina (gah-YEE-nah): hen

gordo (GOR-doe): fat

guapo (GWAH-poe): handsome

guisantes (ghee-SAHN-tehss): peas

guitarras (ghee-TAH-rrahs): guitars

gusanos (goo-SAH-noce): worms

hamburguesas (ahm-bur-GHEY-sahss): hamburgers

helado (eh-LAH-doe): ice cream

hola (OH-lah): hello

jaulas (HOW-lahss): cages

juguetes (hoo-GHEH-tehss): toys

lápiz (LAH-peace): pencil

leche (LEH-cheh): milk

lechuga (leh-CHOO-gah): lettuce

luna (LOO-nah): moon

mañana (mah-NYAH-nah): tomorrow

manzanas (mahn-SAH-nahss): apples

mar (MAHR): sea

mercado (mehr-KAH-doe): market

montaña (mone-TAHN-yah): mountain

mosca (MOE-skah): fly

muñeca (moo-NYEH-kah): doll

músicos (MOO-see-koce): musicians

naranjas (nah-RAHN-hahs): oranges

oso (OH-soe): bear

otra vez (OH-trah VEHSS): again

oveja (oh-VEH-hah): sheep

papel (pah-PEL): paper

peligroso (peh-lee-GROE-soe): dangerous

por favor (POR fah-VOHR): please

procesión (pro-seh-see-OHN): parade

rana (RRAH-nah): frog

rápidamente (RRAH-pee-dah-men-teh): quickly

rata (RRAH-tah): rat

ratón (rrah-TONE): mouse

reloj (rreh-LOE): clock

sapo (SAH-poe): toad

tan bella (TAHN BEH-yah): so beautiful

tan grande (TAHN GRAHN-deh): so big

tenedor (ten-eh-DOOR): fork

tiburón (tee-boo-RRONE): shark

tigre (TEE-grey): tiger

tijeras (tee-HEH-rahs): scissors

tomate (toe-MAH-teh): tomato

tortuga (tor-TOO-gah): turtle

tren (TREHN): train

trompeta (trome-PEH-tah): trumpet

tubas (TOO-bahss): tubas

uvas (OO-vahs): grapes

valle (VAH-yeh): valley

ventana (ven-TAH-nah): window